Winter Blossoms

Paul Iasevoli

Part of
SEASONS OF LOVE
Anthology

Beaten Track
www.beatentrackpublishing.com

Winter Blossoms

First published 2018 by Beaten Track Publishing
Copyright © 2018 Paul Iasevoli

ISBN: 978 1 78645 230 6

Cover Design: Paula Streeter

Beaten Track Publishing,
Burscough, Lancashire.
www.beatentrackpublishing.com

To Bill, my life's love.

Contents

Rise to Fall

I PICKED UP THE phone.

"Robby?" a woman's voice asked.

"No."

The receiver clicked and the line went dead.

It was the third time that week *the voice* had called asking for Robby. It might have been my curt "no" that put her off from explaining any further as to what she wanted with Rob, or "Robby," as she said.

When he came home at five that night, I found the courage to ask about the caller.

"A woman asking for Robby?" He stared at the wall. "Nobody calls me Robby...that I know of."

"Really? Well, she's called three times this past week."

"Maybe she's trying to sell me something."

"Maybe she's trying to sell herself. Where do you go, anyway...those nights I wake up and you're not in bed?"

"The movies...I told you, Chris. I like the late shows at the Prospect—two-fifty and I get to escape from—"

"From me?"

"From myself, and you."

"Fuck you."

"Fuck you!" Rob always managed a louder "fuck you" than me when we argued.

I got off the couch, stormed out the apartment door, and walked the cold, short hallway to the stairs. I ran down the four flights to the street, unsure where I was going.

The corner of Beech and Bowne was dim in comparison to the lights along Kessina Boulevard. I drifted two blocks in their direction like a moth drawn to a lamp. The pink and blue neon street signs shouted in Korean, "*Kimchi gwa Mandu.*" Beneath them, smaller English letters whispered, "kimchee and dumplings."

I walked past the Prospect movie theater, toward the subway station on Roosevelt Avenue, where a hooker clucked her tongue at me as if I would be interested in anything she had to offer.

My night alone in Manhattan would piss Rob off for sure. Either he'd move out and take his dirty laundry back to his mother's house, or I'd tell him he had to leave. I paid three-quarters of the rent, and who needed his seventy-five dollars a month, anyway?

As I climbed down the subway stairs, the smells of alcohol-laced urine and the smoky essence of axle grease mingled with the September night's cool scents from above. I waited on the concrete platform next to mothers holding infants, Hispanic men in heated conversations, and couples speaking Korean. The train pulled up in front of me, tagged in big letters—STAY HIGH 420. In the car, I sat next to a sweet-faced black woman, her hair full of Afro-sheen. She smiled as she scooted over to give me more room. I opened my mouth to say thank you, but my words never formed in the greasy air. I stared across the car—the names "Jose" and "Emmanuel" leaped out at me from the twisting, twirling colors on the opposite wall.

When the Seven train screeched into Times Square station, I nodded to the Afro-sheen woman next to me as I got up first. She gave me a polite smile without a word, as if she understood my haste that night.

Above ground, Seventh Avenue shimmered in a light drizzle. But rather than take the subway, I walked the thirty short blocks to the Village just to blow off some steam.

As I moved south, to the place that used to be my home away from home, I thought about the night I met Rob in the Hamptons nearly six months ago.

***

An early spring crowd of tourists filled the Swamp that weekend. "Rusty, gimme another Cutty and soda," I shouted across the bar. I needed some Dutch courage to talk to the hot, mustachioed man standing next to me. But when the DJ spun Gloria Gaynor's national gay anthem—a song I'd hated since the first day it got airplay on Kiss97—I grabbed my drink and went outside. I smoked a cigarette on the patio and headed to the "old man's bar" behind the Swamp's disco.

A chorus of gray-haired men were singing "Drinking Again," sounding better than Sinatra or any other crooner who'd rendered that tired tune. As I walked in, more than one or two heads turned to look at me. It wasn't often that a swarthy, well-built twenty-something joined their crew. When I broke into the chorus, off-key as I was, the man next to me put a withered hand on my bottom. I whisked it away, like I would shoo a fly from my coffee, and went on singing about telling jokes to jokers and laughing at broken hearts.

A tap on my shoulder turned into a grip that forced me around. I looked into gunmetal-gray eyes, and something told me right then and there to run away. His eyes and sandy mustache would keep me captive if I let them. But I didn't run as I should have. Instead, I stood dumbfounded, like a pubescent boy who'd experienced his first wet dream. I was new to all of this—new to this chase and conquer. I had always been the outsider, a window-shopper never buying.

"You come over here to hide from me?"

I looked up from my drink and studied the long, lean man I'd stood next to at the disco bar just moments ago. I mumbled something about the music in the club being too loud and gulped my Scotch and soda.

He gave me a throaty laugh. "You older than you look?"

"I'm twenty-four," I said, spitting out my age within earshot of men who could have been my father. "Name's Chris—Chris Winter."

"Rob," he said, and motioned to the bartender. "Markey," he yelled. "Two Cutty and sodas."

"I got a full drink."

"Ah...you'll need another soon enough. You want lemon?"

I nodded, not sure I liked lemon in my Scotch.

"Twist or wedge?" Markey asked.

Rob turned to me.

"Don't matter," I said.

Markey pushed the drinks with lemon twists over to us. He held up his hand when Rob offered him a twenty. "On me," he said.

Rob tucked his money back into his billfold.

"You're friends with Markey?" I asked.

Rob shrugged. "He never makes me pay when I come into the old man's bar."

"You're a regular? Then how come I've never seen you here before?"

Rob picked up his glass and took a swig. "Only come out here once a month from Queens to check on my property."

"You got property out here on the East End?"

Rob took a long sip of his drink before he answered. "Not really. It's in Mastic Beach—I rent out my house there in the summer."

"Mistake Beach." I laughed at the nickname of that hamlet through my haze of Scotch.

"What's that supposed to mean?"

"It means what it sounds like—that town is a dump."

Rob lifted his glass and let out a throaty laugh. "That it is, but it makes me some good money from the couple of queers I rent it to—it's their cheap Fire Island."

The chords of "Skylark" rang out, and the gray-haired men singing dampened our attempt at idle conversation until our glasses were emptied, and Rob's lips were on mine.

Markey whistled from behind the bar when Rob took me into his embrace. It might have been my imagination, but the men around the piano gasped as Rob led me out the door to the patio.

That night, we didn't make it back into the disco. Instead, we headed straight to the back of my Pontiac. The leather seats were cold against my backside as Rob took off my pants. It was dawn when we were done, and Rob asked me to see him again. Maybe he could come to my apartment in Queens, or we could have dinner someplace on Northern Boulevard.

I nodded yes and kissed him. My first tryst with a man who looked like he'd stepped out of a Marlboro ad was better than I'd ever dreamt.

***

The rain on Seventh Avenue draped a veil over the memory of my first night with Rob. When it turned into a downpour, I ducked into the nearest bar on Christopher Street to avoid looking like a wet rat.

"Heart of Glass" played on the jukebox, but the din from the Friday night crowd drowned out Debbie Harry singing about love being "a pain in the ass."

I asked for a Scotch and soda—no brand names in Boots and Saddles. A man had to be butch in that place and not priss-it-up by ordering any fancy libations. Meanwhile, the conversation from two leather men standing next to me was something about choosing the right cornice for their windows that faced out on Twenty-Sixth Street.

Overhead, fat Christmas lights spun and twisted in flashing colors—strung up year-round, they were Boots' poor excuse for a disco ball the joint couldn't afford. I looked around at the scruffy men at the bar and asked myself what I was doing there.

I slugged back my Scotch and headed out to the street where I waited under the ragged awning for the rain to stop—September showers in Manhattan never lasted for more than an hour as they worked their way out to Long Island.

Once the downpour withered to a trickle, I turned and walked a half block west on Christopher toward Ty's. When I stopped under the rainbow flag to step inside, the smell of pizza caught my nose, and I decided I was more hungry than thirsty.

I crossed the street and waited in line outside Big Slice Pizza Parlor—the place was packed at nine-thirty on a Friday night. I studied the crowd inside, flaming queens and leather men sat together holding hands next to chic uptown couples all enjoying the biggest slices of pizza the city had to offer. In the corner, a man sat at a table with his back to me, his broad shoulders and sandy short-cropped hair caught my eye. He held the hand of a thin woman across from him. When she saw me staring, she nodded, and the sandy-haired man turned around. My heart skipped a beat.

Rob got up, ran out the door, and through the line. "What're you doing here?" he said.

"Getting pizza." I nearly spit the words in his face. "How'd *you* get here…and who's the fish?"

Rob's eyes darted to the blonde at the table inside. "That's my…sister."

"You always hold hands with your *sister* when you have dinner?"

Rob grabbed my arm. "C'mon in and meet her."

"Bullshit!" I pulled my arm from Rob's grip. "Is she the bitch who calls you 'Robby'?"

He forced a throaty laugh. "Could be," he said. "C'mon in and meet her, you might like her."

I bolted away from him and ran up Christopher across Seventh Avenue to the corner of Sixth. For the second time that night, I was running from the only man I'd ever invited into my life. I needed to get far away from the West Village, away from Rob and his "sister."

At the corner, I hailed a cab and asked the driver to take me to Stix Nightclub at the foot of the Queensboro Bridge. There, I would be halfway home, maybe see some friends I knew from high school on Long Island.

The yellow cab pulled to a stop in front of the gray, box-like building. Outside, the music throbbed as I paid the doorman five dollars to get inside.

I nodded with the beat of a song I'd never heard. Its lyrics were Caribbean, but its rhythms synchronized with the desperation of gay men living in early 1980s New York City.

I was in the middle of a head bob when a short, brown man came up behind me.

"You new here?" he asked in a heavy Spanish accent.

My head continued bobbing, ignoring his question.

"I'm Xavier," he said. "You like to make love?"

I turned to him and said, "*Vete pa' el carajo.*"

"Oh, you speak Spanish?"

"*Coño...claro,*" I said.

"You got a filthy mouth."

Then I kissed him. Kissed Xavier with a vengeance. Next thing I knew, we were making out on his couch someplace in Bed-Stuy, miles away from the Seven train. Miles away from Rob. Miles away from my moral sensibilities. Miles away from any decency.

"I have to go," I said before Xavier could get me into his bed.

"But why? You don't like me?"

I pulled on my shirt and buttoned up my jeans. "I'm faithful to one man."

On the street, I darted past shuttered Brooklyn buildings and down into the bowels of the nearest subway station. The fool in me had let a good-looking trick slip through my fingers. I zigzagged my way north to Queens, changing trains three times. Being born on Long Island had its privileges, but what city kids lacked in fresh air and green grass, they made up with street and subway smarts—two things I never had.

As I climbed the four flights up to my apartment on Beech, the sun shone through the transoms above the landings. Rob worked Saturday mornings, and I could sleep the day away. When he came home, dinner would be ready, and I'd serve him as if I were June Cleaver whether or not he deserved such pampering after the fight we'd had and my growing suspicions.

A stew pot simmered on the stove when Rob called from work on Saturday afternoon. Avoiding any talk of the previous night's argument, he told me how his boss at the electronics factory wanted him to take the train out to the Hamptons and stay overnight. It was the boss's wife's fiftieth birthday, and there would be fireworks. I could come out if I wanted to, but I'd have to get a hotel room—an impossible task on such short notice, even after tourist season.

I told him not to worry. I would put the stew in the fridge and get some take-in Chinese. He thanked me for my understanding before he hung up.

That bastard. I bet he's with his "sister."

Sunday morning, I woke up early, reached for Rob, and remembered what he'd said—he was at a birthday party and would be home later. After I flipped through the *Daily News*, I made a coffee, and watched Sam Champion's rainy weather report on Channel Seven.

When I heard the key turn the deadbolt in the door that dreary afternoon, Rob had that "I have something to tell you" look on his face—a look I'd come to hate in the months we'd lived together—it always meant he was hiding something.

"What?" I asked before he could speak.

He stared down at the floor, never glancing up at me. "I came home to change," he said, "but I have to go right away. My mom's making Sunday dinner."

"Sunday dinner," I echoed.

"Yeah, you know, sauerbraten and all the trimmings."

"I suppose…"

"C'mon, Chris." Rob's voice pleaded with me not to get mad at being left alone again.

"No, no," I said. "You go on to do what you have to do. I'll be here waiting. Your *sister* going to be there too?"

Rob shook his head and went into the bedroom to change clothes. He kissed me on the forehead before he went out the door. "See you later," he said.

I waited up that night as late as I could. At ten-thirty, I went to bed but kept one ear cocked to listen for the deadbolt to unlock.

It was after midnight when Rob climbed into bed next to me. I could smell the perfume on his neck—Chanel No. 5— the same fragrance my mother used to wear. I wondered if that were what his "sister" wore as well. I pushed the thought out of my head and slept until the alarm buzzed at six a.m. I made a coffee after I'd showered, shaved, and dressed. Another day at Queens College teaching punctuation lay ahead.

Before I left, I looked from the kitchen into the bedroom. Rob was still asleep on his day off. His sandy mustache fluttered with his snoring breath. He was the Marlboro Man I'd dreamt of finding, so if he had an occasional fling to satisfy his other needs, I could take that in stride.

***

When I got home from work, I thought it strange that the deadbolt to our apartment was unlocked. I pushed it open and called for Rob. The rustle of fabric from the bedroom first caught my attention, then the sight of Rob in his boxers greeted me.

"Wow, you're home early," he said.

"Half a day today. You know I only teach one class on Mondays."

Rob's face went red. "Oh, I forgot."

"Robby, what's going on?" a woman called from the bedroom.

"Nothing…sis," Rob said.

"Sis?" *the voice* asked.

I looked at my "Marlboro Man" with a jaundiced eye. "Your sister?" I bolted for the door.

He grabbed me by the shoulder. "It's not how it looks."

I shook myself free, hurried down the four flights to Beech Street, out to Kessina, and toward the subway station at the end of Main. Pink and blue lights flashed above me but, with my mind racing, I didn't recognize their words or their signs.

I drank my way from bar to bar, until the Manhattan evening turned to a blur of yellow cabs and sulfurous streetlights. I caught the last express train back to Queens and climbed four flights to face the man I thought I loved.

Rob was on the worn-out couch in the sitting area we called a living room. In the six months we'd spent together, we'd made love there more times than I could count.

He swirled the Scotch in his glass. "It's late," he said.

"Yeah, too late," I said. "Have to get up early tomorrow. I have two classes."

Rob nodded. "Let me explain."

"Explain what? That you used me to get out of your mother's house? Needed me to pay rent you couldn't afford? Wanted me to suck your cock?"

Rob stared out the window toward the brighter lights of Kessina Boulevard. "No, it's not that, it's—"

"It's that 'sister' of yours!"

Rob looked down into his Scotch and nodded. "Maybe," he said.

I blocked him out for the five minutes he droned on about orgies, bondage, water sports, and sex acts I'd never heard of nor understood. And imagined myself with my thumbs pushing in on his Adam's apple until he gasped for air. I would gaze into his gunmetal-gray eyes until they turned beet red, unclench my grip, and watch him fall dead to the floor.

"Did you hear me?" Rob asked.

I nodded, although I had no idea what he'd said.

"So if you want to find me, I'll be at the house in Mastic. Call me there when you decide what you want to do."

He went into the bedroom and pulled his suitcase from underneath the bed. Dresser drawers slammed closed with a hollow sound. The zip of his suitcase echoed through the sitting area, and wheels rolled out behind him to the front door.

I turned and stared out the window toward Kessina Boulevard. The suitcase rattled over the threshold and the door latch clicked.

"See ya," I shouted at the metal door once it closed.

***

After my breakup with Rob, I waited until mid-October to hit the bars again. On a warm, fall afternoon, I drove out to the East End. Sunday tea dance at the Swamp was what the old queens called "the fish fry," since it was the only day the club allowed in women and straight couples.

With the disco packed, I perched on the upstairs landing. From there, I could ogle the shirtless eye-candy moving on the dance floor. When a spot opened at the bar, I went down the stairs. "Rusty, a Cutty and soda," I hollered through the din.

Rusty held up a lemon wedge in his right hand and a twist in his left. I pointed to his left. He slid the icy glass to me, I left a five in its place, and took a seat with my back to the dance floor and the door.

It had been three weeks since I'd seen Rob. I didn't really miss him, although I did miss the sex. I swirled the ice with the Scotch in my glass, watched the lemon twist follow the cubes on the bottom, and remembered how I'd wanted to kill Rob the night he said he needed me *and* his "sister" to satisfy himself.

It's a good thing I wasn't drunk that night or I just might have done it. My picture would have been on the cover of the *Daily News* with a headline reading: "Homosexual Strangles Boyfriend in Fit of Jealous Rage." I imagined what my mother would have thought—worse than that, Father Jim at Saint Francis's Catholic Church. All the *Our Fathers* and *Hail Marys* in the world wouldn't have saved me from eternal damnation. Not to mention my subsequent confinement on Riker's Island.

The smell of cumin and musk exuding from somewhere at the bar distracted me from my daymare of Hell and prison life. I sniffed around to find out who it was that smelled so strange. Tight back muscles glistened on the shirtless man beside me. I pushed my barstool out to move a few feet away when the sweaty man turned to me.

"Chris!"

"Xavier?"

"You alone?"

I was in no mood to have a conversation with an almost-trick I met weeks ago at Stix, let alone put up with his heady scent. "What're you doing here on a Sunday afternoon, all the way from Brooklyn?" I asked as if I cared.

"Oh, a friend of mine from Mastic invited me to come out. So I took the train to Shirley."

"A friend from Mastic?"

"Yeah. He's out on the patio with his girlfriend, Linda. Come outside and meet them."

The patio seemed a more refreshing option than sitting next to Xavier indoors taking in his odor. I followed him into the bright light filtering through oaks ready to lose their golden autumn leaves.

On a bench, with their backs to me and Xavier, sat a man—his sandy-hair somehow familiar—and a blonde girl so slender she seemed made of matchsticks.

"Robby," Xavier called across the patio.

With the fall sun warming my back, I froze up inside. Rob turned and smiled when he saw me. I looked left, then right, wondering which would be the better escape option. The urge to wrap my hands around Rob's throat and murder him surged in me again. I swallowed that thought and my pride. "Hi," I said, as I studied the skinny girl next to him. "And this must be your sister." I extended my hand to the blonde.

She never reached for it. Instead, she turned to Rob and gave him a puzzled look.

He let out that throaty laugh of his, and I felt my stomach tie into a knot.

"No…not my sister. This is Linda," he said.

"Oh, I see," I lied as if I understood.

"I thought you knew each other?" Xavier asked.

"We used to," I said. "At least, I thought I knew *him*."

Linda looked from me, to Xavier, then at Rob as if she were watching a ping-pong ball bouncing off a table.

Rob patted the seat next to him. "Come sit," he said.

I sat on the wrought-iron stool. Its hummingbird and flower pattern pinched and pricked at my backside.

Xavier untied his shirt from his waist, buttoned it up over his bare chest, and took a spot across from the three of us.

I need a shot, a joint, a Valium...anything to get me through this farce.

"So, how've you been?" Rob said as if we were standing next to an office water cooler on a Monday morning after a long weekend.

"How have I been?" The words slithered through my teeth. "I've been in a 'fuck you' mood with everybody since you left."

Linda's eyes turned the size of muffins rising in an oven.

Rob laughed.

God damn it, I want to rip that laugh from you. I want to tear your vocal cords out.

"Why you so angry?" Xavier asked, as if he'd read my mind.

"I'm not angry," I said, mitigating my true feelings. "Hurt, I think is a better word. Hurt by a half year of lies."

"They were never lies," Rob said.

"Yeah, I should have surmised…"

Linda's eyes had sunk back into her head until that point, but bulged up again, like someone added too much baking powder to the muffin mix. She shifted on her stool. "Well, I don't mind it," she said.

"Don't mind what?" I asked.

Xavier nearly spit his drink across the space between us. "Boy, you dumb."

"I must be. Who are you, anyway?"

"Xavier's one of my summer tenants in Mastic," Rob said.

I glared at Xavier.

He grinned.

That laugh of Rob's sounded again, louder than before. "He knew who you were that night at Stix. I'd told him about you, showed him your picture, told him how good you were in bed, and he wanted to try you out for himself."

The urge to rip Rob's Adam's apple from his neck came over me again, but I checked my rage and stood up to leave.

Linda grabbed my arm. "Where're you going?" she asked. "I think an afternoon with three men like you would be much more fun than only two."

My eyes spun 180 degrees from Linda, to Xavier, and to Rob. I slammed my drink down on the low, wrought-iron table of hummingbirds and flowers next to me. "You all are into something I want no part of."

"Aw, live a little—take a walk on the wild side," Rob shouted as I stormed away. His throaty laugh carried down the path to my Pontiac in the parking lot. I kept the windows of the car rolled up and blasted the Police's "Wrapped Around Your Finger" through the stereo speakers. I must have rewound the cassette five times to that same track in the two hours it took me to drive home to Queens that evening.

Numb November

THE CRISP NOVEMBER night invigorated my steps down Kessina Boulevard. From Roosevelt Avenue, I took the Seven train into Times Square, switched to the Seventh Avenue Local, and climbed out at the Christopher Street subway station. I cruised down the gleaming tar-covered, cobblestone street peering into plate-glass windows of bars along the way. Men in leather bomber jackets, their fur collars matching mine, looked back at me with lecherous eyes, but I ignored their stares. After my breakup with Rob, the last thing I needed was another cheap trick using me to satisfy his whims.

When I reached the Hudson River Drive at the far end of the West Village, I turned right. On my left, streetlights shone above the broken waterfront docks. I thought about the many men who'd fallen to their deaths at that spot, unreported by the *New York Times* or *The News at Six* on Channel Seven, their insipid lives unworthy—an everyday occurrence in 1980s New York City.

The wind picked up and I pulled my collar higher around my neck. I needed a drink, a stiff shot of Scotch, to keep me warm. The El running the length of the Drive broke the breeze somewhat, hanging derelict above the pavement like the skeleton of a dead elephant that a zookeeper neglected to remove from its cage. I scurried through its bones to a redbrick building. The black sign that marked my final destination creaked its name—"The Anvil." I pushed open the chalky-black door to a bar I'd never visited.

"Ten dollars," the pudgy doorman said.

I unzipped my jacket and reached for my wallet in the right inside pocket. As I thumbed through the money in my billfold, the doorman ran his hand over my pectorals bulging through my white T-shirt. I whisked his hand away as I gave him a ten.

He smiled at my reproach. "For you, I'll make it five tonight."

I didn't argue and switched the ten for a five. Whatever money I could save on a college teacher's salary would mean the difference between steak and tofu that week.

After my half-priced admission to what I was told was the hottest bar on the West Side, I tucked my wallet into my back pocket and checked my jacket at the door. I'd brave the drafty club in my T-shirt for the night. The cold air only added to my pectoral attraction, my nipples pointing hard through the cotton fabric. When I leaned up against the big, square bar and called for a drink, a muscle man next to me didn't hesitate to pinch my teat. I winced and stepped away. "Cutty, straight-up," I yelled to the bartender again.

He answered me with his middle finger and went back to mixing his regular customers' drinks. Undaunted by the barkeeper's gesture, I waited for my turn to be served.

I let my gaze drift around the bar while I waited. *Oh, no. Not Xavier...God, not that almost-trick from Stix. He's like a bad penny. Tell me it isn't so.* Next thing I knew, Xavier was waving to me across the thin early Friday evening crowd. *God, don't let him come over to talk to me.*

He picked up his drink and walked to my side of the bar, his cumin-laced, sweaty scent invading my privacy. "Hi," I said and feigned a smile.

He sucked the dregs of his drink from the bottom of his glass. "Haven't seen you since that afternoon in the Swamp when you ran away from Robby and me."

"I've been busy," I lied and looked away.

"With what?" he asked.

"With classes…and other things."

"Like tricks?"

"Like it's none of your Goddamn business," I said.

"You know, you are what we call *un esnob*."

I nodded and thumbed my nose in the air.

Xavier threw his head back, gave me a defiant stare, and disappeared somewhere into a darkened corner of the club. The bartender slapped his hand in front of me.

"What'd you need?" he asked.

"Cutty straight—make it a double."

He poured a double shot of Scotch into a tumbler glass and held up a strip of lemon zest. "Twist okay?"

I nodded.

He pushed the glass to me. "Sorry about giving you the finger before, but—"

"You were busy."

He smiled and extended his hand across the bar. "Name's Samuel."

When I shook his hand, I was sure he could feel me trembling. "Chris Winter," I said.

Samuel patted my hand. "Call me if you need anything."

I cast an embarrassed grin down at the bar top and nodded into my full drink. Samuel's clear-blue eyes and bright-white smile certainly were something of an enticement, but deep down I recognized a gigolo when I saw one.

I took a walk around the club. The wood-plank flooring was standard for that kind of place in New York City and carried into the toilets. I cruised into the bathroom. The stained oak planks were covered in sawdust to absorb the urine and whatever other bodily fluids might fall on the filthy floor. Early as it was, the toilet action, that earned the Anvil its reputation, had yet to begin. At the trough, I relieved myself, just in case it got busy later and I'd be deprived of any personal space where I could pee.

I left the bathroom and headed to a far corner of the club. I leaned against the wall, hoping that Xavier wasn't somewhere lurking in the dark. By ten o'clock, the lights on a stage at the club's back wall lit up and began to twirl. Leather men and shirtless muscle boys bellied up to the stage. I moved to a seat at the bar and turned to face the show. I had no idea there would be live entertainment that night, but if my five dollars covered it, I was going to get my money's worth.

The swirling lights went out, and the entire club went pitch-black. A hand groped my ass. I grabbed it and pushed it away. The stage lights came back on and twirled again. In a spotlight's beam, Xavier stood naked on the stage, a tub of Crisco next to him. A barrel-chested man picked up a two-feet chain with three-inch links and greased it from end to end. Xavier bent over onto his hands and knees and moaned as the burly man shoved each link into his rectum until the chain completely disappeared.

I felt my Scotch climb into my esophagus and ran into the nearest toilet. Two men stood at the trough masturbating. Not wanting to throw up on the floor, I puked between them, breaking their momentum.

After my spontaneous vomiting, I made a beeline for the coat-check. I gave the boy behind the half-door a dollar, grabbed my jacket, and pushed my way past the pudgy doorman. Out on the street, the cold November air cleared my head somewhat. The wind blowing through the El whispered to my ignorance—*a night in a gleaming city is not as it seems.*

I crossed beneath the dilapidated El and headed to the Hudson River docks. The glow of streetlights cast my shadow across the rotted beams leading out into the river. With the collar of my jacket pulled up over my chin, wind-driven pins of ice stung my cheeks and ears. I let the breeze take my caution with it, and stepped onto the first treacherous beam. It creaked and groaned under my weight, the second splintered but held its shape. I took giant-steps over gaps between the plank logs until I came to a shipping container hanging precariously halfway in the water. The sulfurous light barely lit the inside of the rusted tin shack. I flicked my Zippo and lit a cigarette, its dull-red glow illuminated the space, its tilted metal floor strewn with used condoms and cigarette butts. I added my half-smoked Marlboro to the pile at the entrance of the container. But, with cold needles piercing my ears and nose, I decided I was wasting my time on a dark November night. I turned and walked back through the skeleton of the El glowing yellow above the West Side's roadway.

By the time I'd crossed the pavement to the opposite side of Hudson River Drive, the wind had found its way underneath my jacket. With a shiver running up my spine, I pushed the chalky-black door of the Anvil open and waited in the short line that had gathered in front of the pudgy doorman. When it was my turn to get into the club, he looked me up and down. "You again," he said.

I nodded and brushed past him.

He grabbed me by the fur collar of my jacket. "Yo! You need to pay."

"What?"

"You didn't get stamped on the way out."

"But you know I was here less than an hour ago. You felt up my chest, and now you don't recognize me?"

Still gripping my collar, the doorman got off his stool, and dragged me to the door. The other patrons—all in leather jackets waiting to get inside—jeered as I went flying by.

I shook myself from the fat man's grip. "Wait a minute," I hollered. "I'll pay the ten dollars."

The doorman held his hand out and waited for my money. With a glint of victory in his eyes, he waved the bill I gave him in the air and bowed to the other men in line.

I hung my head as I walked past them, my face redder from embarrassment than from the cold wind outside. In the club, I kept my jacket on, albeit unzipped. I found Samuel at the bar and waved to him. "Cutty, double, straight up," I called. Rather than give me the finger, this time he smiled as he poured my order and handed it to me.

"You look like shit," he said.

"Gee, thanks."

"Where'd you go? I saw you run from the bathroom out the door."

"Out for some air."

Samuel laughed. "Any action in the air on the docks?"

I shook my head. "Too cold," I said and put a five on the bar. Samuel shoved it back.

"On me. I caught a glimpse of Tommy's little show with you at the door."

"Oh, that…"

Samuel grinned. "He loves to play that game with newbies. Don't let it bother you."

I shrugged. The guy next to me slammed his hand down on the bar top between Samuel and me. "You bitches done talking so I can get a drink?"

"Hold your horses, cunt, I'm getting to you next." Samuel gave me a wink. "See ya later, Chris," he said.

I stepped away from the bar to make room for the thirsty patron breathing down my neck. I walked around the club as it was filling up. The lights on the stage lit and swirled to signal the start of the eleven-thirty show. If it were going to be anything like the ten o'clock, I really didn't want to watch.

I found a nook that held a recessed door, its deadbolt locked tight. I nestled into the little cove. From my angle, I couldn't see the stage or the performance. A tall man with pockmarked skin found his way next to me in my secure resting spot. He pulled a joint from his pocket, lit it, took a hit, and offered me a toke. I took a swig of my Scotch, wiped my lips on my sleeve, and inhaled a deep drag of the harsh smoke. I nodded my thanks to the man when I handed the joint back to him. He took another hit and offered it to me again. I shook my head—one toke of pot with a tumbler full of straight Cutty was more than I needed to get me through the night.

Music thumped from the stage across the bar bouncing off the beams of the small nook I stood in. I leaned on the door behind me and let the vibrations run up my back. The alcohol and THC filtering through my brain let me float into a fantasy where I felt myself a part of the entire building, as if I were a structure anchored into the shallow bedrock of Lower Manhattan. Adrift in my euphoria, I heard someone shout, "Can you fucking move, dickhead?" Someone was pushing me aside. I spun around. The doorman stood next to me. He unlocked the recessed door that had been my support and switched on a light that lit a staircase to a basement.

"Jesus H. Christ, kid," Tommy said. "You have been one pain in my ass tonight."

I stepped aside and looked toward the man who'd let me share his joint.

He smiled and shrugged.

Tommy climbed down the stairs and the pockmarked man followed behind. I peered into the basement, wondering what was down there. When more men in leather jackets descended the stairs, I was piqued. I looked over to the bar and spotted Samuel. I had to ask him what went on downstairs before my curiosity got the better of me.

"Samuel, another Cutty, but with soda this time," I shouted above the thumping din. He handed me my drink. I got a five out to pay, but before Samuel took the bill, I grabbed his hand. "What's downstairs?" I asked.

"Just another bar—quieter than up here." He plucked the five from my fingers, and rushed over to the next man who shouted for a drink.

Quieter was what I needed after getting pushed and shoved around for the past two hours. I followed the narrow stairs down into the basement. The smoky air from the upstairs club mingled with the musty scents of damp concrete. The basement's walls were nothing more than rough-hewn stone, its floor a reddish sandstone worn smooth by what must have been two hundred years of steps. The man I'd met upstairs motioned for me to sit next to him. I pulled a stool over and moved closer to the bar. He took another joint from his pocket and offered me the first toke. I took a hit and drew the smoke deep into my lungs. "Thanks," I coughed, "but that's enough." He nodded, but looked at me blankly as if he didn't understand.

"Chris," I said and offered him my hand.

"I no English," he said as his grip tightened on mine. "Me Russian—Ivan."

Even though I could speak five languages other than English, Russian was not on my list. I smiled and nodded. "Nice to meet you," I said.

Ivan answered with a blank stare and took the last hit off his joint.

A hand slammed the bar top in front of me. Tommy's pudgy face was in mine. "Where'd you get that drink," he snarled.

"From Samuel upstairs," I said.

"Well, finish it quick, bitch. Down here, you buy your drinks from me."

"Why you so rude?" I yelled. The buzzing in my head forced my voice to ring across the small, rectangular bar.

Three leather men at the opposite side laughed. "That's the way Tommy shows he likes you," the middle one said.

Tommy put his hands on his hips and turned to face the three. "Don't be giving away my secrets, bitches," he lisped to the leather men.

"The new kid is cute," a man at the rectangle's corner hollered. "We'll see what he can do in the backroom later."

I downed the Scotch and soda in my glass and ordered a Cutty straight.

Tommy poured my drink and handed it to me. He grabbed my wrist before I could reach into my coat pocket to pay him. "On me, kiddo," he said. "Thanks for being a part of the show."

"Show?" I mumbled.

"It's all a show," Tommy whispered and turned to serve the new customers coming from upstairs.

I patted Ivan on the shoulder and got up to make room for the other men waiting for drinks at the bar. I knocked back my Scotch and walked away to explore the basement that was more cave-like than the quiet lounge I'd understood from Samuel's brief description. Tucked into its dim-lit corners were wooden benches and metal stools. In one small alcove, a rubber swing hung by chain links from the ceiling. I turned a corner and tripped into a passageway. A thick layer of fresh sawdust broke my fall and masked the smells of urine and semen that lingered in the air. I stood up and brushed myself off. I followed the narrow passage until I walked into a pitch-black wall. I took out my Zippo and flicked it to light my way lest I trip and fall again.

A hand reached out from the darkness and grabbed me by the nape of my neck. "You do that again, I'll rip your heart out and piss on it, you jackass."

It might have been the side effects of the Russian's pot, but I went into a panic. As I hurried away from the sinister grip, I risked flicking my Zippo again to get my bearings and ran toward the light of the downstairs bar. Before I made it out of the dim passageway, two hands grabbed me by my shoulders.

"Chris, where're you going?" I couldn't see the speaker's face, but his voice was somehow familiar.

Still in panic mode, my mind raced. *Who down here would know my name—fuck, not Xavier?* I reached into my pocket for my Zippo to light the face that spoke to me. But not wanting my heart ripped out and pissed on by a man I didn't know, I hesitated to strike it.

Then a kiss—warm and gentle—worked its way up from my neck to my ear. "It's me, Samuel," the voice whispered and pressed me against the rough-hewn wall. He held me in his embrace as we melded together in the sawdust on the sandstone floor.

Christmas Crisis

O N A MID-DECEMBER Friday night, the wind whistled down Kessina Boulevard as I walked to the Roosevelt Station. Having taught two classes at Queens College that day, I was exhausted, but the end of the fall semester merited a night out in Manhattan. Besides, I hadn't been to a bar since that night at the Anvil back in November.

A light snow flurried down the subway steps, melting to a glisten on the treads leading to the Seven train's platform. I got out at Times Square station and strolled over to Broadway to check out the Christmas windows at Macy's. The crowd of onlookers blocked my view from the newest displays of boys riding in tandem on sleighs and reindeer leaping over skyscrapers—their hooves nearly touching towering roofs that mirrored the New York skyline. Rudolf led the sleigh above The Twin Towers—Santa's last drop-off point before he crossed the river to deliver gifts to the good boys and girls on the mainland.

I put aside my frustration at not being able to see more of the windows and stepped from the sidewalk into the street. Better to give the opportunity to children, so they could see what America was made of at Christmastime—materialism with a tinge of religious irreverence.

When I hit Thirty-Third Street, I made a right toward Seventh Avenue. In the middle of the block sat O'Sullivan's, a dive Irish Pub I'd visited the previous Christmas season. It still had a smoking section and was the only place not packed with tourists that time of year. Besides those two perks, O'Sullivan's oyster stew was the cheapest and the best tasting in the city.

A year later, the memory of the creamy concoction's pleasure made my mouth water in anticipation. When the waiter came to my table, he gave me a puzzled look. "You waiting for somebody else?"

"No, I'm alone."

He clucked his tongue. "Pity," he said as he took my order.

I nodded when he turned and walked away. Yeah, a pity that Rob and I couldn't last through the holidays, but as autumn froze into winter I didn't miss him, nor did I miss anyone else's company. After six months of waiting around for a man who only showed up when he felt like it, I enjoyed my solitude.

The stew arrived, and I devoured it along with a glass of sauternes. I scraped the last bits of creamy brine from the bottom of my bowl and called the waiter over for the check.

"Something else?" His crisp-blue eyes and blond hair made me long for dessert.

"No," I said, belying my inner thoughts.

"Very well, then." He turned to walk away.

"Wait a minute," I called. *What are you doing later?* my heart said, but my lips parted with the words, "An amaretto, straight up."

"Right away," the waiter said.

I bit my tongue with my foolish shyness. I should have asked him—I should have given up my stupid pride. What did I have to lose? The worst that could happen would be he'd tell me to go fuck off if he were straight. I lit a cigarette and waited for my drink.

"Anything else?" he asked when he delivered the amaretto to my table.

I shook my head, and he handed me the check. I slipped two twenties into the fold and held it in the air, but before he took it from me, I asked, "What's your name?"

"Joe."

"Chris." I shook his hand and let my brown eyes melt into his blue. "I'll be down on piano row later, if you're off."

Joe gazed around the nearly empty restaurant. "By the looks of it, we'll close by eleven. Where you gonna be?"

"I usually hang out at Marie's Crisis, provided it's not packed with tourists for the season."

"Might see you there." Joe patted me on the hand when he took the fold. "Any change?"

"No, that's for you."

***

When I left the restaurant, the wind howled from Thirty-Third down to Penn Station. I thought about taking a cab to the Village, but the queue for taxis stretched all the way to Thirty-Fourth Street. I figured by the time I got into the warm, smelly confines of a yellow cab, I could be halfway to my destination. I pulled the collar of my bomber jacket over my chin and braved the icy, winter chill.

In Chelsea, I stopped to study the mannequins in Barney's windows along Seventh Avenue—all male, dressed in festive reds and greens, their crotches pumped up, as if the winter weather had no effect on the size of their external genitalia. I crossed over Fourteenth Street and walked nine more blocks to Grove Street. The line I expected to find at Marie's was nil, but Rose's Turn was packed to the gills. With Momma Blake playing there that night, the crowd was clamoring to get inside.

I popped open the door of Marie's and went down the short, narrow stairs. Their balustrades were hung with silver and gold snowflakes that carried down the rails and back up again across the low ceiling in regular patterns. *Albert, the manager's work,* I thought—*it always takes a sissy to make something pretty.*

The piano player sat at the upright, arranging his songbooks for the night, as the sparse crowd milled about. Albert stood in front of a mirror in the small back coatroom adding the final touches to his makeup.

As I hung my jacket on a corner hook, John, the Quebecois bartender called to me, *"Salut, Chris, ça va?"*

"Bien, mon p'tit chou," I said.

"Cutty avec soda ce soir?" John asked.

"Oui," I hollered back. That summer I'd spent at the University of Laval perfecting my French came in handy if I ever needed a quick drink from any stray francophone I might meet.

At the bar, John kissed me on both cheeks and pushed my Scotch to me. "So how you been, *putain*?"

"Anything but," I laughed. "There ain't no whoring for a woman left lonely."

"I heard about that Rob you were seeing."

"What?" I shrieked loud enough to force Albert to turn away from his makeup mirror. "How'd you know about that mistake?"

"This is a small big town," John said, "and news travels fast from the Hamptons to Manhattan."

I threw my head back and clucked my tongue. *"P'tit monde."*

John nodded. *"Vraiment, mon ami.* I heard most of the story from that *putain,* Xavier."

"That fuck," I said. "Last time I saw him, he was getting a two-feet chain shoved up his ass at the Anvil."

"And Rob's not any better. He's got a reputation as a playboy, you know, but more than likely you didn't know *that* when you met him. *Dommage.* You had to find it out the hard way."

I looked down at the floor. "I let him fuck me over—"

"C'etait pas ta faute. You didn't know…but next time…"

I took the bartender's hand in mine and kissed his palm. *"Merci, mon cher."*

***

Thirty years my elder, John L'Eauclaire was my gay Dutch-uncle. Right after I came out, Marie's Crisis was the first gay bar I visited in Manhattan. That night, John poured my drinks for free, as he explained the history of the mirror running the length of the wall behind him. With the words, *Liberté, Egalité, Fraternité* etched into its copper and silver finish, covered in protective Plexiglas, the mirror was said to be a gift from Lafayette himself to the original 1820s owners of the house on Grove Street.

After a long night of drinking, and an even longer history lesson from John, my head pounded the next morning. I swore I'd never go back to Marie's again, but the following Friday, I sat across from John drinking—only difference was, I went home with an empty wallet on that second visit.

***

The piano player's trill over the keyboard forced my memories of John to trickle away, as Albert let out a shrill vibrato, "La, la, la…" to get the early crowd's attention.

I moved from the bar and took a seat next to the piano.

"Well, boys, what'll it be to start the night?" the music maker asked.

Men on stools around him mumbled titles of different shows they may have done in high school—where they played a tree or a silent soldier, but never sang a note. While they searched for a title, I shouted, "Something from the *Fantasticks*."

The short, squat piano player smiled at me and pounded out the first major C chord of "I Can See It."

I didn't dare sing Matt's tenor part, I left that to a blond *ingénu* next to me. But when the time came, I belted out El Gallo's warnings of deception and big city despair. By the middle of the song, I was in a duet with the young blond at my side, but I got lost as the tempo picked up, and the piano player had to jump in to help my weak vocals through to the harmonic end. With all our flaws, the boy and I got a round of applause for attempting a difficult song to start the night.

When the couple next to me asked for a tune from *Bye Bye Birdie*, I got up and walked over to John.

"*Je pars*," I said.

John scrunched his brow. "You're leaving so soon?"

"I need a smoke and some air, beside I hate this show."

He leaned over the bar and kissed me on both cheeks. "*A bientôt, mon ami*."

"By the way," I said, "if a cute blue-eyed guy named Joe comes in asking for me, tell him I'm next door at Rose's."

"Joe?" John shouted over the rising chords of "Normal American Boy."

I nodded to him and waved to Albert through the silver and gold snowflakes on the stairs.

***

I lit a cigarette in front of Rose's Turn and got in the line that had shortened somewhat over the past hour. Either people had given up waiting in the cold or they were inside pressed shoulder to shoulder against the walls.

Nonetheless, Momma Blake was worth the wait. Rumor had it she was a great-niece of Eubie Blake, something she refused to confirm or deny. Her talent was certainly akin to the great Eubie's—what other singer would ever attempt to craft a blues rendition of Blondie's "Rapture"?

As I waited, the December wind found its way under my jacket, and I pulled it tighter around my waist. A young, uptown, straight couple in front of me gave up their spot and headed back to Seventh Avenue. I took two steps forward and waited for the doorman to check the IDs of five people ahead of me.

From behind, an arm wrapped around my shoulder. I turned and met face-to-face with two crisp, blue eyes.

Joe grimaced. "Ain't you cold?"

I feigned a deeper shiver than I really felt just to have him pull me closer into his embrace.

"What the fuck you out here for?" he said as he wrapped his other arm around me.

I pulled myself from his grip. "It's Momma Blake playing tonight—"

"Oh, fuck that," Joe said. "Come on down to Marie's…at least there's heat and plenty of room there."

I hesitated to give in to a man whose last name I didn't even know, but I nodded and followed him into Marie's where Albert held the door for us.

"So, bitch," Albert said when he saw me, "you've decided to come back and join the gay world."

I smirked at his dull wit and handed him a ten to cover the entrance for me and Joe. He pushed the bill back to me. "You were here just a half hour ago. Give the tip to the piano player, or better yet get a drink for yourself and your new beau."

I put my arm around Albert's thick waist and kissed him on his chubby cheek.

He pushed me away. "Now don't go messing up my makeup, bitch. Just go downstairs with your pretty blond and drink lots of drinks."

Joe flinched when Albert pinched his ass as he walked past. I grabbed Joe's hand, and we went over to John at the bar.

"*Mon cher*," John shouted. "Cutty and soda?"

I held my palm up and turned to Joe. "What do you want?" I asked.

"Scotch is fine."

I nodded to John. "*Deux.*"

"*La meme, deux fois?*"

"*Oui.*"

John looked over my shoulder, spotted Joe, and winked. When he reached for the bottle of Cutty sitting under the word *Fraternité,* he gave me a stealthy thumbs-up. "*Tu as de chance avec lui,*" John said as he pushed the drinks across the bar.

"Maybe," I whispered in John's ear and handed him the ten Albert had refused at the door. I passed the Cutty and soda to Joe. "John's a friend from way back."

Joe nodded. "I can tell. You two always speak French?"

I smiled. "It's our little game. It keeps the tourists guessing if John and I are really lovers…it's all a show."

"A show?" Joe put his lips to his glass and took a long sip. "Like you inviting me here tonight?"

I grasped his free hand and squeezed it in mine with the gentlest of grips. "No, there was nothing fake about asking you to join me here."

The chorus around the piano was singing a tune about a trip somewhere over the rainbow when I took Joe into my arms. I held him close and pressed my lips against his. Next thing I knew, his tongue was in my mouth and we were grinding against each other.

John slapped his hand on the bar, and Albert sang in my ear, "Break it up, young lovers, before you go too far, and I have to throw you both out of my bar."

Joe and I pushed away from one another and laughed at the musical interruption.

"These friends of yours are too much," he said.

I stared down at the floor and took another gulp of my drink. "Friends," I slurred from the effects of exhaustion, alcohol, and walking in the cold night air. "I really don't have any."

"I've lost most of mine," Joe mumbled.

"What?"

Joe shook his head. "Never mind."

We went over to the piano where I put a dollar in the tip cup along with a request for "Ol' Man River." When the piano player finally got to my song, I made a feeble attempt at Paul Robeson's version of the *Showboat* tune, but in my less than sober condition, my voice cracked like eggs falling to the floor.

Joe looked me up and down. "Are you drunk, Chris?"

I nodded, then shook my head. "More tired than drunk," I said. "The holidays…the cold…it all wears me down."

"Let's get out of here. I don't think you need anything more to drink. You want a coffee?"

I agreed and bid *adieu* to John and Albert. Joe held my hand through the silver and gold snowflakes on the stairs, out the door, and into the cold wind blowing across Grove Street.

We passed Rose's Turn and ducked into the New Moon Café—the favorite coffee shop of every gay man who'd drunk too much on a night out in the West Village. We grabbed two stools at the bar where Michael was both waiter and barista.

"Chris—Joe," he said. "What are you two doing here… together?"

I looked at Joe.

"We're not here like that…well, together…yes," Joe said, "but not like *together*…"

I scrunched my brow. "Well, maybe later," I blurted out.

Joe frowned and ordered two cappuccinos.

Michael nodded and went to the espresso machine to brew the early morning coffees.

I wobbled on my stool.

"Chris, my place is just over on Tenth. We can go there and—"

"And what?" I ran my hand down Joe's chest.

He stopped me before I could reach his waist. "And you can sober up on my—"

"*Café, Signori!*" Michael put two frothy cups in front of us interrupting Joe's thought.

I straightened my back and took a sip of the steamy drink, hoping its warm caffeine would sober me. I locked eyes with Joe's and ran my hand over the light stubble on his cheek. "Listen," I said. "I'm still on the rebound… I'm sure you don't want to hear about any of that, but my heart's still broken."

"Still broken?" Joe's mellow tone turned angry. "Whose heart's not been broken in this fucked-up world we're living in? My lover, Tim, died a year ago from the 'gay plague' that's going around. How do you think I feel? Not a single friend that Tim and I had wants anything to do with me—they're afraid they might catch it too. And who knows, they may be right. I might be the next to die from a disease that doesn't even have a name."

I wrapped my arms around Joe and pulled him close to my chest. "I know…I understand…I just broke up with my boyfriend after six months, so—"

Joe pushed me away. "Oh, bullshit," he shouted. "Don't even try to compare a six-month boyfriend with the five years I spent with my Tim. We were happy…now everything I had is gone."

I looked away, searching for words that would ease the bitterness raging in Joe's eyes.

He took one last sip of his coffee and got up.

"Don't go," I pleaded.

Joe shook his head. "No, it's time I leave. This ain't gonna work." He hurried out the door of the cafe. I followed after him, but the flurries from earlier that evening returned as a steady snowfall and blocked my view of Joe's direction.

Downy white muffled my footfalls along Grove Street. I stopped in the middle of the block and considered walking over to Tenth to search for Joe and at least give him my number. But instead, I turned back toward Seventh Avenue. On the corner of Sixth, I hailed a cab to Times Square station and caught the Seven train back to Queens. The snow along Kessina Boulevard covered my shoes as I walked home to my apartment building.

I curled up in my bed, and Joe's blue eyes filtered into my mind as I drifted off to sleep. In a half-dream, we rode a sleigh down a slope in Central Park. Joe's arms wrapped around my waist as I glided us to a stop on a flat, smooth stretch of packed snow.

"Thanks for the short ride," he said. "Too bad your sleigh won't fly."

New Year Promises

WATCHED 1983 SLIP away on the TV screen with a bottle of Korbel Extra Dry at my side. Once the ball dropped over Times Square, I downed one last glass of champagne and clicked off the set. I stared out the window toward Kessina Boulevard, where revelers shouted and firecrackers burst under the pink and blue neon signs along the street. I lit a joint and took two long hits before I clipped the roach and let myself drift into a reverie of what 1984 might bring.

That Orwellian-numbered year was something I'd thought about since high school. Would Big Brother be watching over my shoulder as Reagan set fire to the Evil Empire? Could we survive another term of his senile rambling State of the Union addresses? Would the CDC deal with the epidemic sweeping the nation?

I lifted the champagne bottle to my lips and sucked the last drops of its dregs. A new year in which I'd turn twenty-five. Another year alone. I thought of Joe, and how his eyes filled with rage at the memory of his dead lover and the government's lack of concern. And how his anger kept us apart that night we'd spent in the Village. Did I blow my chances with another man because of my naivety?

I pulled the shades down in the bedroom and cuddled under my down comforter. Tomorrow would dawn a new day—a new year, where I could look Janus-faced and move in a different direction.

***

My first week back at Queens College started with a freshman class crammed with the usual shining faces—boys and girls just a few years younger than me. All eager to learn the difference between a period and a semi-colon. All longing to be the next Fitzgerald or Hemingway. I gave them my standard first assignment's writing cue: *My winter break was full of____*. Inevitably, a class clown in the back of the lecture hall called out, "Shit." And I had to give the obligatory eye-roll and cluck my tongue. "So, three hundred words," I said, feigning my re-composure. "That's one full page, double-spaced, written on a standard Remington or Royal typewriter."

In the back of the room, a handsome, dark-haired boy's hand shot up.

"Yes," I called on him from the lectern.

"What if it's more than three hundred?"

"More than the word limit and you will lose points, so be precise—tightness matters."

"Like those pants you're wearing," I heard a snide, blond jock whisper from the far end of the first row.

"What was that, sir?" I stared him down.

The boy, not more than nineteen, turned red with surprise at my keen hearing. I cleared my throat and continued explaining the assignment. "It's due by Monday, so go home and get to work. Try to surprise me, and you just may end up on the cover of the *Sunday Times*."

As fifty feet shuffled out of the lecture hall, I sat at the small desk next to the lectern and marked my plan book with what was ahead. Nothing more than reading some poorly written assignments and struggling to discover one or two that deserved to be copied and distributed among the class—essays that had either major flaws, or a rare gem to be polished for possible publication.

How many of those gems had I written myself when I was a teenager? All of them with inclusions, but none of them rare enough to be acquired by an agent or major magazine.

I threw my pencil down on my plan book and reflected on the three hundred words I would write about my winter break. A night wasted in the Village, a blue-eyed man who turned on me, a drunken spree on Kessina Boulevard where I drank sake and ate so much kimchee I puked for two days.

I stuffed my plan book into my leather satchel, headed to the lecture hall's doors, flicked out the fluorescent lights, and walked across campus to Jamaica Avenue. I took the Seven train up to Roosevelt and went back to my empty apartment on the corner of Beech and Bowne.

***

When I met my Monday freshman class the following week, I collected the papers on the cue I'd assigned. Each was clipped and double-spaced following the format I'd outlined on our first class meeting. After I had all twenty-five in my hands, I read the hook lines in their first paragraphs. I didn't read the names, just their first sentences.

"'It was a cold and snowy break, filled with icy wind,'" I read and looked out on the sea of shining juveniles. "Reactions?"

"Trite."

"It's been done before," another voice called.

"Ditto, trite," I said.

"Jane Austen–like," a girl from the back yelled.

"Nineteenth century indeed," I said.

I flipped through five more papers and began to read one that caught my attention.

"'I thought the night I met Rob would be full of love. I was in the Village at a club called the Eagle's Nest. It's a dark and mysterious place, where the men all dress the same, like they just walked off a stock movie set in Hollywood. Rob stood out in the crowd, his steel-gray eyes, light-brown hair, and...'" I stopped and held my breath. "Who wrote this?" I mumbled.

I looked around the lecture hall, pulled myself together, and called, "Reactions?"

"Brilliant."

"Uniquely original."

"Redundant phrasing," I said, "but true."

The dark-haired boy who'd asked about writing more than three hundred words sat in the back of the hall—his eyes downcast, his chin in his hands. "And you, sir?" I said pointing to him.

He picked his head up.

"What do you have to say?" I asked.

"A nearly true story," he called across the hall.

"Ladies and gentlemen, I give you case in point. A story from the heart is the essence of good writing."

A murmur went through the class.

"Today we adjourn with this. Next time we meet, I want you to read pages 119-230 of the Chicago Manual and be ready to apply it to an in-class practical. I will also have your papers back by next Monday. Good day, be good, and... smoke 'em if you got 'em." My last line got its usual laugh as my students emptied the hall.

When I came home that late afternoon, I pulled out the dark-haired boy's paper, whose name my class records indicated was Gonzalez, and put it on the top of my pile for review. Could it really be the same Rob of my six-month affair?

I re-read the lines I spoke in class earlier that day.

I thought the night I met Rob would be full of love. I was in the Village at a club called the Eagle's Nest. It's a dark and mysterious place, where the men all dress the same, like they just walked off a stock movie set in Hollywood. Rob stood out in the crowd, his steel-gray eyes, light-brown hair, and tight blue jeans certainly were an eye-catcher.

I tried to ignore the fact that he was the hottest thing in a bar filled with men who looked like they belonged on the cover of American Bear Magazine.

I walked away from the steel-eyed man. My heart still pounding when I went to order a Bud—hoping the bartender wouldn't ask for my ID again that had the five of 1965 altered to a two so I could get into the Eagle at eighteen. The hairy-armed barkeep didn't ask for my license and handed me a tepid Bud. I chugged it back and walked the perimeter of the square bar where men twice my age ogled me.

I ordered another beer and settled into a corner, when a hand crept down my pants and grabbed my rear. I whirled around, ready to smack whomever it was, but when I looked into the feeler's steely eyes, I melted straight away. Nonetheless, I raised my hand in a threat. He gave me a guttural laugh and grabbed my arm.

"You new to this place?" he asked.

I stared him down through the dim light. "Not really," I lied.

He laughed a deep, chesty laugh again. "Well, then, you should be used to getting felt up."

Not wanting to seem the outsider, I nodded, and gave him my name, "Georgy."

"Rob," the steel-eyed man said and pressed his lips to mine. "You want another Bud?" he asked when our lips parted.

"Sure," I said.

Rob called to the bartender, and the beer was next to me in a second. Next thing I knew, he forced me to chug another. After he pressed me to down a third, he told me to follow him into the toilet to take a piss. I suppose it was the alcohol that made me do what I did, but when I left the Eagle, my throat was burning from the effects of uric acid, and my clothes stank of stale urine.

On the subway ride home, I sat alone on a corner seat until my stop in the Bronx. I ran back to my apartment on Conduit Avenue, ripped off my shirt and blue jeans, and tossed them down the garbage chute.

A winter break full of piss was something I'd rather forget about.

My stomach retched when I read the last lines. That son of a bitch Rob. How could he do that to a boy nearly half his age? The amoral bastard.

I considered the comments I would make on Gonzalez's paper. He was over the limit by nearly one hundred words, but the realism of the story was worth the extra reading. Should I put a "see me," note on his paper? Should I pull the kid aside and tell him not to degrade himself again with anyone like Rob? No, I would leave the personal out of my critique and grade him as I would any other student.

He'd lose ten points for going over the word count and a point for every grammatical error—of which there were few that I noticed. Of course, my blind eye to the paper helped the total score. I would also take off another five points for the repetition of the trite use of "steel eyes"—although I knew it was an accurate description. How could I fail a student who'd been brave enough to put a bad experience into an essay and hand it to an English instructor he didn't know? In green ink, I gave the assignment a score of eighty.

I pushed aside Gonzalez's paper and went on to read a girl's account of a ski trip in the Adirondacks. Her father had paid for a stay at an exclusive lodge, and the snow was perfect—"so full of cold-white fun…"

I read to the middle of the page, gave her a green grade of ninety, and went to bed.

***

By week's end, I'd finished my Queens College tasks. All the assignments read, all the grades noted in my ledger, and the following week's classes planned out, so I decided to reward myself with a night out in Manhattan. I tugged on my 501 button-fly jeans and tucked the cuffs into my leather work boots. I pulled a sweatshirt over my white cotton T-shirt and grabbed my bomber jacket out of the narrow hallway closet.

As I rode the train into the city, I thought about Rob and mulled over various ways I'd exact revenge on him for what he'd done to me and how he'd used Gonzalez. Maybe a penknife into his back, or perhaps I could lure him to the docks along the Hudson. I would push him into the cold, swift-moving current, and he'd end up decomposing on a beach in the Bronx.

As the train made its last stop at the Hudson River Railroad Yards, I set aside my murderous thoughts and climbed the stairs up to Thirty-Fourth Street. From there, I walked along the river's edge to the Eagle's Nest. At ten o'clock, a long line of men waited to get inside—all looking to cop a feel someplace in a dark corner of the club, or maybe get pissed on in the backroom's oversized, porcelain bathtub.

The doorman waved me in. My good looks and city garb must have been to his liking. When I stepped inside, the place smelt of sweat, stale urine, and burnt hemp, mingled with a hint of patchouli air freshener. I bellied up to the dull-black bar and ordered a Scotch and soda. I wanted to be halfway sober if I were to run into Rob at his usual Friday night hunting grounds.

Although I'd visited the Eagle many times, I still found it the strangest bar in Manhattan. It had a DJ but no dancing was allowed. In a black booth on the back wall he spun tunes that never got any airplay, as men, all dressed in obligatory leather, walked in circles. Reminiscent of a scene from *Midnight Express*, they'd stare at each other with lustful eyes. One would stop to grope the other and move on to the next.

I made the rounds. Not seeing Rob, I parked myself at the bar. The keeper came over to me. "Another?" he asked.

"Cutty, but make it straight with a lemon twist," I said over the DJ's throbbing mix. I grabbed my drink and put a five on the bar. I got up to take another stroll around the busy club. And there he was, Rob, with his hands inside the pants of the man who'd served me dinner just a few weeks before Christmas. I took a slug of my drink and walked up behind the two of them.

"Copping a good feel?" I said over Rob's shoulder. "Or is he trying to mend your broken heart?" I snarled into Joe's ear.

They whirled around and glared at me. Joe stepped back from Rob and buttoned up his fly.

Rob adjusted himself in his jeans. "What're you doing here?"

"Not the same as the two of you." I locked eyes with Joe. "So, this is how you ease your pain of lost love and mourning?"

He diverted his gaze from me to Rob.

Rob let out that throaty laugh of his. "Always the intellectual. Can't you just suck a dick and forget about it?"

"Can't you ever think past your crotch?" The three of us made a triangle with me at its apex. I felt for the penknife in my pocket. If I were to do what I had thought about, I would surely be the loser—my three-inch blade wouldn't even make it through the outer lining of Rob's bomber jacket.

Rob shoved his face closer into mine. "Get lost, you little fuck. Why don't you go back to your Queens' apartment and read a book?"

My frustration at overload, I splashed my drink—Scotch, ice, and lemon twist—into Rob's gunmetal-gray eyes.

His face dripping, he lunged at me, but Joe held him back.

"Just go away," Joe said. "Just get out of our space."

"Fuck you," I shouted, "fuck the both of you." I stormed away and strode up to the bar. "Cutty, double, straight up," I hollered to the nearest bartender.

I grabbed the glass, hid it under my jacket, and hurried out the door. On the street, I lit a joint and smoked it until the roach burned my fingertips. I leaned against the Eagle's cold, brick outside wall and sipped my drink to cool my throat. The THC and alcohol eased my shivering from the rage boiling inside me.

With my head buzzing, I knocked back the dregs of my Scotch, smashed the glass on the pavement, and walked south along Hudson River Drive in the direction of the Anvil.

"Chris?" a voice called from somewhere under the El. Through the sulfurous light, I thought I recognized the man who'd made love to me two months ago in sawdust chips on a sandstone floor.

"Chris," he shouted again.

I focused on his face, not sure it was really him—his crow's feet made him look a little older—but when he kissed me, I recalled Samuel's gentle lips.

"Where're you going?" he asked.

"The Anvil," I slurred. "I'm looking for something... somebody."

"Like who?" Samuel gave me a puzzled stare. "You lose something?"

I shook my head.

"Look, I just got done with my six-to-eleven shift at the bar. I'm going to the Eagle. Come along."

"I was just there," I mumbled.

Samuel took me by the hand. "C'mon, we'll have a drink."

I followed him, not knowing if I could stand up much longer after too much Scotch and a whole joint.

Inside, Samuel ordered a beer and asked me what I wanted. "Coke with ice," I said and reached for my wallet. It dropped from my hand, but Samuel caught it in midair. I fumbled trying to get my money out and dropped it again. Samuel picked it up off the floor.

"You know what?" he said. "Let me hold on to this. You're in no condition…" He grabbed the drinks through the crowd that had built up at the bar. "You okay?"

I shook my head. "No, I'm not. My ex is here…up to his old tricks. He's like Big Brother…always watching." I gulped my Coke, hoping it would dilute the alcohol running through my brain. "It's like he knows…knows the men I've been with."

Samuel put his arm around my shoulder. "Chris, you know you're not making any sense?"

I nodded. "Maybe not, but…"

"C'mon, let me get you out of here."

Samuel grabbed my elbow. We walked to the street and got into the first yellow cab cruising down Hudson River Drive. I turned to him in the back seat and grinned. "Where're we going?"

"Back to Queens," he said. "To the address on your license—210 Beech Street. Is that right?"

I nodded and passed out.

My eyes slit open when the cab stopped on the corner in front of my apartment building. Samuel helped me out of the backseat. "You're home," he whispered. In the hallway, he put his hand in my pocket and fished out the deadbolt's key.

**

Saturday morning, the sun shone through my bedroom window. I must have forgotten to pull down the shades. I rolled over. A warm man snuggled next to me. I sat up with a start. "What the fuck!"

Samuel laughed. "How's your head?"

I put my hands to my temples and groaned.

"That good, eh?" he said.

"How did you…we…?"

"Taxi."

"What! How much did *that* cost?"

"Twenty-five dollars," Samuel said. "It was either that, or risk losing you in the gap on the subway platform, and that wouldn't have been fun. How'd you get so fucked up anyway?"

"Too much pot. Oh God…did we…?"

Samuel grinned. "Not with the condition you were in. Now lie down, and I'll get you a cold cloth for your head."

When he got out of bed, the tighty whities he wore accentuated his firm butt and V-shaped torso. He went into the bathroom, and I heard water running. Samuel came out with a wet washcloth in his hand. "You got ice?"

"Why, you thinking of making a drink?"

Samuel clucked his tongue. "No, stupid—for your head."

I pressed the wet cloth to my forehead and mustered a chuckle. "I know…in the freezer. I'm sure you'll find it with the size of this place."

"Your apartment's a palace compared to mine in Manhattan."

He came back into the bedroom with three ice cubes in his hand, took the cloth from my head, and wrapped them inside. "Better?" he asked.

I nodded and scrunched my brow. "Why are you doing this for me?"

Samuel ran his hand over my bare chest. "Because I like you…because I saw something in you that first night at my bar in the Anvil. Not only a pretty face, but you're not a jerk." He lay down next to me and pressed his lips to mine. The three ice cubes tumbled out of the washcloth and melted between us.

***

The late January sun had nearly set that Saturday when Samuel stepped out of the shower and dressed. "I got the six-to-eleven shift again tonight," he said as he walked out of the bedroom into the sitting area.

"Oh." I looked out the window toward the lights flickering to life over Kessina Boulevard.

Samuel grabbed my chin to force me to look at him. "But I'm off tomorrow."

"Really?"

"You know, Chris, 'really' is not what you're supposed to say. How about, 'would you like to get together?' or something like that? Well, I really would, so here's my number." He handed me a slip of paper.

I stood up and put my arms around him. "I'm sorry I'm such a dope. It's just that…I never thought a man like you would—"

"Would fall in love with you at first sight? Well, I did. Sometimes good shit happens when you least expect it." Samuel kissed me hard. "So what do you say we get together for dinner tomorrow night?"

"Dinner would be nice."

"Finally a correct answer." Samuel smiled. "Just come into Manhattan and ring the bell on the box next to the entrance at Ty's—apartment three is mine."

"What time?"

"Five okay?"

"Five it is, then." I threw my arms around Samuel's neck and kissed him. When he went out the door, I ran to the window and watched him fade away in the dim streetlight on the corner of Beech and Bowne.

Valentine Vows

SUNDAY AFTERNOON, I took the subway into Times Square station and switched to a downtown train. As I climbed the stairs up to Christopher Street, my heart pounded. Would Samuel keep his promise? Would he answer the bell when I rang apartment number three?

A cold wind blew in my face, but I plodded down the block looking forward to a new adventure. My relationship with Rob was the first I'd ever had, if I were not to count locker room encounters with high school seniors when I was just a freshman. They'd let me suck them off after gym class and go back to tell the older boys that they'd found a queer slut in the school's basement. If I refused to do as they asked when they came downstairs, I'd end up with welts I couldn't explain away.

I suppose that's why I buried myself in books. I read *Catcher in the Rye* five times trying to figure out if Holden Caulfield were a latent homosexual—much to my chagrin, he turned out straight. And then there was Hemingway— why did he shoot himself? In my opinion, *The Big Two-Hearted River* revealed his sexual ambiguity through the use of Jungian archetypes. When I presented that idea to my eleventh grade English teacher, he scoffed at me. "Ernest Hemingway was a big game hunter—a man's man—and *you* think he was a homosexual?" The class laughed at me, and I was put to shame for the rest of that school year.

But in senior year when we read *In Cold Blood*, I wagered that Capote was homosexual. My teacher, Mr. Field, had a tendency to agree. "A man with Capote's turn of phrase," he said, "must see the world from a different angle." And there were many different angles that Mr. Field and I saw together—like the brother's habits in *The Glass Menagerie*. Where did Tom really go on those nights he said he was "at the movies"? All those memories flew through my head as my finger hovered over the buzzer to Samuel's apartment above Ty's.

After I overcame my initial hesitation, I pushed the button labeled "three."

"Chris?" Samuel's smooth voice sounded through the speaker.

"Yeah, it's me."

"I'll be right down," he said.

I folded my arms as I waited in the January chill blowing off the Hudson. Samuel bounced down the stairs like Tigger longing to greet Pooh Bear. I pushed him back when he planted a wet kiss on my mouth.

"Not here," I said, "in the middle of the street…in broad daylight."

Samuel pulled me in closer to his face. "Oh, fuck that!" He slipped his tongue into my mouth, stepped away, and laughed at my blush. "You wanna walk?" he asked.

"Are we going local?"

"Well, I was thinking Auntie Maude's up on Forty-Fourth."

"Are you nuts?" I scowled. "I'm not walking forty blocks in this cold."

"I could keep you warm along the way."

"No, that's okay, I'll pay for a cab."

We walked arm in arm along Christopher to Sixth Avenue and grabbed a taxi uptown. We got out on the corner of Forty-Second Street and hurried past the porno houses leading to the Theater District.

Auntie Maude's was nearly empty at six on Sunday evening. The theater crowd had gone to see their matinees, and the gay clientele was either napping or primping for the evening.

Samuel chose a table next to a small window that looked out on the street.

The waiter, most likely an off-off Broadway actor, brought us our menus. "Drinks, gentlemen?" he asked.

Samuel looked at me. "You drink wine?"

"Sometimes," I said.

"Well, would you share a bottle with me?"

"Yeah, okay."

"Red or white?"

"I think I might like white." I guessed at my preference.

Samuel looked up at the waiter. "A bottle of Mouton Cadet, Maine et Sèvre."

"Very good," the waiter said.

I squinted at Samuel. "Where'd you learn to pronounce French like that?"

"My mom was Belgian. I heard French around the house when I was a kid. I can still understand it, and I can fake it if I have to."

"I have a Master's in French," I mumbled.

"What?"

"I have a degree in French…not that it's done me any good."

"*Really.*"

The waiter brought the bottle of wine to the table, uncorked it, and poured two glasses. Samuel and I toasted to our first dinner together.

"What is it that you do, anyway?" Samuel asked to break the silent pause between us.

"I teach English to wannabe writers at Queens College."

"I'm impressed."

"You'd be *de*pressed if you knew what it's really like. I read bad English all day long and try to right the world with proper grammar."

"Sounds pretty boring, I have to say."

I took another sip of my wine. "And you?" I asked. "What do you do, besides tend bar?"

Samuel looked out the window. "That's what I do—tend bar."

"Can't be," I said. "How is it that you afford that apartment over Ty's? Even that place must cost a fortune in this city."

Samuel swirled the wine in his glass. "My parents were killed by a drunk driver ten years ago. I got a good settlement when I was eighteen. Since then, I've been a free spirit—was even engaged for a while."

I took a gulp of my wine. "To a woman?"

Samuel laughed. "Well, of course. I might as well be up front with you. I'm bi."

My mind raced back to that autumn afternoon with Rob, Linda, and Xavier. Suddenly the soft-leather seats in Auntie Maude's felt as uncomfortable as the hummingbird and flower metal stools on the Swamp's patio.

Samuel reached across the linen tablecloth and grasped my hand. "You okay?"

I shook my head, but when I looked into Samuel's eyes, I nodded. "It's just that…my first boyfriend was bi. At least, he was screwing his girlfriend and me at the same time."

Samuel squeezed my wrist. "Look, just because I can love both sexes doesn't mean I don't want to be monogamous. When I fall in love, it's with one person at a time. I loved the girl I was going to marry, but *she* fell out of love with me."

The waiter came to our table and interrupted Samuel's next thought. "Gentlemen, ready to order?"

I looked at Samuel. "I have no idea."

"Well, the steak is always good here." Samuel closed his menu. "I'll have the New York Strip, rare, with a side of fries."

"Very good," the waiter said.

I looked down at the menu that had turned into a blur. "You know what, let's keep it simple. I'll have the same."

"Coming right up."

We both stared out the window at the traffic and passersby on Forty-Forth Street, until my laughter broke the silence.

Samuel caught my eye. "What's so funny?"

"Well, I'm sure the waiter found that gauche."

"What?"

"Here we are drinking white wine and ordering steak."

"Fuck that. We drink what we like."

I picked up the bottle and filled our glasses.

Samuel took a long sip of wine and squeezed my hand in his. "So, you okay with what I just told you?"

"I'm fine. This is the first time I've enjoyed another man's company in a long time, especially the company of a man who looks like you."

Samuel raised his glass to clink with mine. "Well, that makes two of us."

When our steaks arrived, both perfectly done, we devoured them with voracious appetites. Samuel looked down at his plate and picked up a french fry. "You have to work tomorrow?" He popped the fry into his mouth.

"I have one class, but it doesn't meet till ten."

"In that case, you can come back to my apartment and…"

I lifted my glass to my lips. "You foolish schemer, I thought you'd never ask."

"Hey, chalk one up for Chris! You finally got an answer right."

"I only use my talents on men who appreciate them."

The waiter came back to our table. "Dessert, gentlemen?"

"No," I said. "I have all the sweetness I need in front of me."

***

We grabbed a cab on Seventh Avenue and rode south as January's twilight glinted off the lower Hudson. When we got out on the corner of Christopher, I hesitated. "You want to go to the Monster for a drink?"

Samuel shook his head and grinned. "I have something else in mind."

From the gleam in his eye, I understood his intent. I recalled what he told me at dinner and froze in the middle of the block.

He pulled me closer. "What's the matter?"

"I don't think I can…"

"Why? Don't you trust me?"

Rather than express my true consternation, I shook my head. "No it's not that…It's just that…I've never done anything like this before."

"You've never had dinner with a man and gone home to his apartment for a drink?"

I shook my head again.

Samuel stared directly into my eyes. "Look, Chris, I'm not forcing you. If you want to leave, we can make it another time."

I nodded that it was okay and took his hand in mine.

When we came to the doorbell panel in front of Ty's, Samuel entered a code and pressed the buzzer. I followed him up the narrow stairs to the third floor.

He unlocked the door and flicked on the entranceway light. "It's not much." He pointed to the sofa on the short wall. "Have a seat."

I sat down on the middle burlap cushion of his couch.

Samuel pressed his lips to mine and kissed me firm and hard. When he let go, he grinned his bright-white smile. "What do you want to drink?"

"You got Scotch?"

"Cutty okay?"

"My Scotch of choice…but I think you should remember that."

Samuel went into the corner kitchenette, and I heard the crack of an ice-cube tray. "Lemon?" he called.

"Don't bother," I said, "my lemon days are over."

"Oh, how poetic."

I laughed as he handed me the drink. "There's a story behind lemon in my Scotch."

"Do tell." Samuel set his glass on the small, round coffee table.

I took a swig of my drink. "You don't want to know, but someday I may write about it."

"Well, that'll give me something to look forward to—Chris, and the Story of Lemon in his Scotch: part one...or would it be part two?"

"Shut up!"

"Make me—"

I put down my drink and kissed Samuel's full, red lips, ran my hand through his thick, blond hair, and let my fingers work their way to his crotch.

He pulled me closer to him. "I want you inside me," he whispered. "I've wanted that since the first night we met."

I thought about our first time together in the backroom of the Anvil, and how I let Samuel take the lead—little did I know he would treat me as his equal.

He pulled off his pants as I unbuttoned my jeans. We pressed against each other, throbbing in desire. I licked his chest and he moaned in pleasure until my mouth found its way to his erection. I tasted his sweet saltiness, and he begged for more.

"Not yet," I said.

Samuel got up from the couch and turned out the lights. He held my hand and led me to his tiny sleeping area.

I eased him back onto the bed. With my erection already wet with pre-cum, I gently entered him. He gasped as we thrust together in perfect rhythm. I felt him quiver under me. I released myself, and we collapsed into each other's arms.

Samuel kissed me full on the mouth. "Don't go tonight," he said.

"Only tonight?" I whispered.

"Tonight…tomorrow…never."

I propped myself up on my elbow. "You know, I never believed in love at first sight—"

"Until now." Samuel cut off my thought.

"Until now," I echoed. My lips pressed against Samuel's warm, soft mouth, and we entwined again, until we lay in the sweat of a second orgasm better than the first.

***

The last week of January, I floated in a mist of emotional ecstasy. Samuel would spend his nights off in Queens with me, and when he worked his shift in the Anvil, I would watch TV in his apartment until he came home. From his window, I'd see men my age holding hands or arguing on the street and fill in their dialogue with words I couldn't hear. From time to time, I thought I saw Rob, Xavier, or Joe—all passing through the sulfurous light like phantoms that I let go once Samuel came into my life.

The second to last day of January, Samuel was off. I had no classes to teach the next day, so we went to 88 at the foot of the Manhattan Bridge for dim sum. The weeknight crowd was sparse, since winter had descended on the city, and we enjoyed half-priced sake and more small plates than we could count.

Samuel downed another shot of fortified rice wine. "I was thinking," he said.

"Uh-oh, this sounds like dangerous territory—you thinking."

"Oh, shut up."

"No, you shut up." I gave Samuel the sly smile that always followed our playful banter. "What?"

"My lease is up in two days."

"And?"

"And…are we in love?"

I downed my sake and locked eyes with Samuel's stare. I stretched my arm across the wooden table and took his hand in mine. "Well, if I told you that you make me dizzy when we have sex, does that count?"

Samuel nodded. "And if I told you that when I'm away from you my stomach is in knots until I see you again, does that count?"

I put my finger to my temple. "Let me see. Dizzying sex, plus knotting stomach, equals…I don't know?"

Samuel shook his head. "Oh, shut up."

"No, you shut up."

We laughed at our exchange.

"So when are you going to move in with me?" I asked.

"Wednesday?"

"That's in two days! You think you'll be able to pack by then?"

"Chris, what do you think I got in that tiny place—some underwear, T-shirts, jeans—"

"Dildos," I interrupted.

"Oh, shut up."

"No, you shut up."

"Make me," I said to end our little game.

I flagged down the waiter, and he pushed a fresh cart of dim sum plates over to our table. Samuel and I each took two different dumpling dishes and ordered another round of sake.

We clinked our shot glasses. "Welcome to life in Queens and the Seven train into Manhattan."

"L'Chaim," Samuel said.

"Salut," I replied.

***

It was a snowy Sunday two weeks after Valentine's Day. I was enjoying a coffee and the morning paper, when the photo of a handsome, sandy-haired, mustachioed man in the *Daily News* caught my eye. He stood next to a mousey blonde. The caption read:

> *The parents of Ms. Linda Messina and the parents of Mr. Robert (Robby) Faust are proud to announce the nuptial of their children. Wedding set for June 17, 1984.*

"Hey, Samuel," I called into the bedroom of our apartment, "get a load of this."

Samuel came into the sitting area in his tighty whities. "What?"

I showed him the grainy, black-and-white photo in the paper.

He scratched his head as he squinted at the page. "And?"

"And this is…" I stared at Samuel's broad shoulders and V-shaped waist. I took the newspaper from his hands and tossed in on the floor. "It doesn't matter," I said and pulled him into my embrace.

About Seasons of Love

Love follows no rules. Like sun in winter and rain in summer, love can blossom in the most unexpected places. This richly diverse collection of stories proves that love is as universal and as varied as the seasons.

The Stories:

- *Tourist Season* – Deven Balsam
- *Machete Betty and the Office Sharks* – Neptune Flowers
- *Once Around Seven* – Ofelia Gränd
- *Winter Blossoms* – Paul Iasevoli
- *Year of the Guilty Soul* – A.M. Leibowitz
- *The Great Village Bun Fight* – Debbie McGowan
- *A Springful of Winters* – Dawn Sister
- *Out of Season* – Bob Stone
- *Seashell Voices* – Alexis Woods
- *Courting Light* – A. Zukowski

Available as a complete anthology (ebook/paperback)
and as individual stories (ebook + longer stories in paperback).

For more information/purchase links, visit:
www.beatentrackpublishing.com/SeasonsofLove

About Paul Iasevoli

Paul is a transplanted New Yorker who now lives on the Manatee River on the West Coast of Florida where he enjoys sunrises and sunsets over the Gulf of Mexico. He holds a Master's degree in Latin-American Literature. Writing has always been his passion. This work is dedicated to his late husband of thirty-four years—William J. Montagne.

Social Media

Website: www.pauliasevoliwords.com
Facebook: www.facebook.com/paul.iasevoli

By Paul Iasevoli

"A Night at Madame Beauseau's." Florida Writers Association Collection, vol. 9. *What a Character.* 2017. https://floridawriters.net/shop/9-what-a-character

"Forced into Freedom." Deep South Magazine. January, 2018. Winner Honorable Mention: *Race in Place.* http://deepsouthmag.com/2018/01/29/forced-into-freedom/

Coming October 2018. "The Manatee Sings." Florida Writers Association Collection, vol. 10. *Where is Your Muse.* 2018.

Acknowledgements

I would like to give a word of thanks to all the people who have helped me get as far as I have in my third career. First and foremost, Rick Bettencourt, who guided me along the writer's road. Debbie McGowan, who encouraged me to write this story beyond the first chapter. Thanks to Susan Yansick who has supported my writing efforts for the past six years. And to my beta readers, Sybille Bruning—*Ich danke dir*; Zach Wichter, my former student who has become his teacher's teacher—*Love you, Kiddo*. And to all the members of the FWA Bradenton group—you've shared my highs and lows, but never let me down. Lastly, to Paula Streeter, my cover designer—your insight into the story brought Samuel to life for Chris.

Beaten Track Publishing

For more titles from Beaten Track Publishing,
please visit our website:

http://www.beatentrackpublishing.com

Thanks for reading!